HOME SUPER HOME

ORCHARD

MEET THE POWERPUFF GIRLS!

Favourite colour: Pink
Aura power: Sponge, broom, stapler
Likes: Organising, stationery, science, punching baddies and doing well at school
Dislikes: Mess, being disorganised
Most likely to say: "Let's go save the day!"

BLOSSOM

Favourite colour: Blue
Likes: Animals, creating computer games, make-up, punching baddies, singing, her toy octopus, Octi
Dislikes: Animals being upset, dressing up in ugly clothes
Most likely to say: "I love piggies!"

BUBBLES

BUTTERCUP

Favourite colour: Green
Aura power: Rocket, tank, submarine, cannon
Likes: Roller derby, fighting, deathball
Dislikes: Dressing up, wussy people
Most likely to say: "Don't call me princess!"

SPECIAL THANKS TO ANNE MARIE RYAN

FOR SARAH LEONARD, SUPERHERO EDITOR

ORCHARD BOOKS
Carmelite House
50 Victoria Embankment
London EC4Y 0DZ

First published by Orchard Books in 2017

A CIP catalogue record for this book is available
from the British Library.

ISBN 978 1 40834 735 5

1 3 5 7 9 10 8 6 4 2

Printed and bound by CPI Group (UK) Ltd, Croydon, CR0 4YY

Orchard Books
An imprint of Hachette Children's Group
Part of The Watts Publishing Group Limited
An Hachette UK Company
www.hachette.co.uk

THE PROFESSOR: The Powerpuff Girls' father, the Professor, was trying to create the perfect little girls out of sugar and spice and all things nice. But when he accidentally added Chemical X to the mix, he got three super cute and super fierce crime-fighting superheroes: The Powerpuff Girls!
Likes: Science, The Powerpuff Girls, creating new inventions in his lab under the house
Dislikes: When things explode
Most likely to say: "How could you hate science?"

THE FASHIONISTAS:
Criminal sisters Bianca and Barbarus (Barbie) Bikini love going on a crime spree!
Likes: Shopping and stealing
Dislikes: Orange prison jumpsuits
Most likely to say: "Evil is back in style!"

THE NARRATOR:

Ahem, and there's me. I'm your friendly narrator. I'll pop up now and again to give you all the gossip on what's going on. Are you sitting comfortably? No? Well then get ready! Honestly, do I have to do everything around here? The book's about to begin! Ready? Then let's go!

CONTENTS

THE TOASTER MONSTER

> *Everyone knows that breakfast is the most important meal of the day. But not many know that toast can be very dangerous ...*

The Powerpuff Girls were battling an enormous Toaster Monster. Its black cord flicked from side to side like a tail and it snapped hungrily at the superhero sisters.

"Time to pull the plug on this dude," yelled Buttercup.

She flew at the monster, pummelling its shiny silver sides with her fists. **BISH! BASH!** But her punches didn't even dent the monster's shiny metal.

The Toaster Monster rampaged through the streets of Townsville. Shoppers dropped their bags and ran for cover, screaming in fright. The Toaster Monster crawled towards an old lady walking her poodle.

"STEP AWAY FROM THAT DOGGIE!" shrieked Bubbles. She streaked through the air, leaving a trail of sparkling blue light behind her. Using her superhuman strength, she scooped up the poodle in one arm and grabbed its elderly owner in the other.

She set them down safely in a park, patted the poodle on the head, then flew back to her sisters.

Working together, the three girls launched a blistering attack on the Toaster Monster.

Bubbles kicked the monster, while Blossom and Buttercup flew around, punching and pelting it.

"You're not the only ones who can turn up the heat!" growled the Toaster Monster. A knob on its side turned. Soon, the mouth-watering smell of toast wafted across Townsville.

Buttercup stopped fighting and sniffed the air. "Something smells good," she said, rubbing her tummy. "I'm actually kind of hungry …"

"Buttercup, stay focused!" shouted Blossom. "It's trying to distract us!"

"Nice try," said Buttercup, narrowing her green eyes at the Toaster Monster. "I didn't want toast anyway. I'm in the mood for a sandwich – a **KNUCKLE SANDWICH!**"

4

SLAM! Buttercup bashed the monster.

"Yeah, and I want chops!" shouted Bubbles. **"KARATE CHOPS!"**

BLAM! Bubbles aimed karate chops at the monster.

The Toaster Monster's red eyes glared at The Powerpuff Girls. "Get ready to feel the burn!" the monster taunted them. It flicked the knob on its side to **MAXIMUM**. Its insides glowed orange and smoke billowed out of the top. The horrible smell of burnt toast filled the air.

"Oh no!" cried Blossom. "We've got to do something before it burns down Townville!"

The monster lurched through the city centre, crashing through shop windows and knocking down signs. It was so hot that its metal glowed bright red.

WHOOSH! Blossom blasted the monster with her ice breath. Sparkling crystals covered the Toaster Monster, trapping it in ice.

"Way to go, Bloss!" cheered Buttercup.

But the monster just laughed and pressed a button on its side marked with a snowflake. "Guess you forgot I had a defrost setting," it sneered. Ice melted off the Toaster Monster and it was back in action. Roaring angrily, it used its power cord to lasso a bus and flung it at them.

"We need a plan," said Blossom, as the girls huddled behind a wall. "I say we lead it out of the centre and use the Omega Formation."

"Um … which one's that again?" asked Bubbles.

"Back the monster into a corner then surround him so he can't escape," Blossom explained.

"Oh, yeah," said Bubbles. "I always get that one mixed up with the Theta Formation."

Blossom sighed. "I don't know why I bother giving these plans names if nobody can ever remember them."

"Plans are for wusses – I just plan to WIN," Buttercup told her sisters. She zoomed up in the air and hovered in front of the Toaster Monster. "Hey, big guy!" she called. "You think you're so hot, but I hear you can't even handle a bagel."

"How dare you!" the monster bellowed. "I can turn **ANYTHING** a beautiful, crisp golden brown – even one of you Powerpuff Girls!"

The metallic monster thundered down the street, chasing after Buttercup.

"YOU ARE GETTING CRUMBS EVERYWHERE!" Blossom shouted. She hated mess!

Pink light glowed out of Blossom and took the shape of a vacuum cleaner.

Her vacuum cleaner aura revved its motor and chased after the Toaster Monster, gobbling up its trail of crumbs.

With Buttercup leading the way, The Powerpuff Girls led the Toaster Monster out of the city centre.

"Down here!" cried Bubbles, pointing to an alleyway.

The girls forced the monster to the end of the alley. Its red eyes darted around, looking for an escape route, but there was no way out.

"You're in a **JAM** now!" said Buttercup.

"You'd **BUTTER** believe it!" said Bubbles.

"Nice one, Bubbs," laughed Buttercup, giving her a high five.

9

The Toaster Monster surged forward, trying to flee, but Bubbles was too fast. She grabbed its plug and swung the cord over her head like a lasso. "Buttercup, catch!" she yelled, throwing the plug flying up through the air.

Buttercup zoomed down and grabbed the plug, stretching the cord out in front of the monster's feet. "Now, Bloss!" Buttercup yelled.

"Here, monster, monster, monster," Blossom called, luring the monster over the tripwire. "Can't catch me! You're just a useless appliance which is going to end up on the scrapheap."

"Is that the best you can do?" Buttercup groaned at her sister's awful taunting. But it worked. The Toaster Monster stepped towards Blossom, and tripped over its lead.

"Noooo!" it shrieked as it fell. As if in slow motion, the huge monster crashed towards the ground. As it hit the floor there was a loud **BANG!** Black smoke puffed out of the monster and its red lights faded.

"That dude is **TOAST!**" Buttercup whooped.

Just then, the monster gave one last gasp. A huge piece of toast popped out and shot into the sky. Higher and higher it soared and then – **CRASH** – it landed on top of a big white house.

The girls gasped.

"Unfortunately, so is our house," said Blossom.

Uh oh, I told you toast can be dangerous. Better stick to porridge ...

DISASTER ZONE

> The Powerpuff Girls' house had become
> ... a flat. The huge piece of toast had
> squashed it flat as a pancake!

"The Professor!" shrieked Bubbles. "We
need to check on him!"

The Powerpuff Girls zoomed over to
their house and searched through the ruins.

"Professor Utonium!" cried Blossom. "Where are you?"

"Hello, girls!" said the Professor, crawling out from where his lab used to be. He was wearing what looked like an inflatable fish tank on his head. He gazed around at the toast-covered house, confused. "What happened?"

"A giant piece of toast crushed the house," explained Blossom.

"I was so busy testing out my latest invention I didn't even notice," the Professor said. "But I can

safely say my patented inflatable bike helmet works!"

> *Well, that was a bit of luck!*

The Professor took off the helmet and inspected the gigantic piece of toast. "At least it's wholegrain," he said approvingly.

Using their superhuman strength, Blossom, Bubbles and Buttercup lifted the piece of burnt toast off the house. Then they wandered miserably through the rubble. The living room was a mess. Pictures had fallen off the walls and the big red sofa was broken, stuffing spilling out of the seat cushions.

Buttercup pointed to the shattered television. "How are we going to watch *Space Towtruck* now?"

The kitchen was just as bad. Doors hung off the cupboards and the dining table had been reduced to a pile of wood. Pots and pans were scattered all over the floor.

Blossom gasped in horror. "I had the kitchen organised perfectly. Now look at it!"

Next they went into their bedroom. It looked more like a disaster zone than a superhero base.

"Oh no!" wailed Bubbles, picking up a torn poster from the floor. It was a picture of her favourite band, *Sensitive Thugz*. "Poor Chance!" she said, kissing the picture of the band's lead singer. Chunks of broken ceiling covered the big bed that the three sisters shared.

Toys and clothes were strewn everywhere. Even Blossom's usually tidy desk was a complete mess.

"Octi!" Bubbles screamed, pulling her purple toy octopus out of the debris. She dusted him off and cuddled him tight.

"Don't worry, girls, I have this under control," said the Professor, stepping over the rubble. "I've called a builder to come and have a look. I'm sure this isn't a very big job."

For a very clever man, the Professor could be surprisingly dim sometimes.

Not long after, a builder strode up to the ruined house. He was wearing a hard hat and a bright yellow vest, and he had pencils tucked behind both his ears.

Whipping a tape measure
out of his tool belt,
he started taking
measurements
straight away.

"Mmm hmm," he
said, jotting something
down after he measured up the kitchen.

Then he moved on to the living room.
He gave a low whistle, scratched his beard
and scribbled something in his notebook.

The Powerpuff Girls and the Professor
followed him into the bedroom.

"Tch!" The builder tutted loudly as he
noted down the measurements.

Finally, they went down to the basement
where Professor Utonium's science lab was
– or, where it used to be.

Glass from broken test tubes was sprinkled across the floor and the Professor's scientific machines had toppled over.

"Humph," the builder grunted, shaking his head. "Tut, tut, tut."

"I don't understand a word he's saying," the Professor said.

"Leave it to me, I'm good with languages," Bubbles told him. She flew over to the builder and hovered in front of him. She cleared her throat delicately, then launched into a series of tuts, heaved a deep sigh and finally gave a wolf whistle.

The builder replied with a long *hmmm*, putting a pencil behind his ear and then scratching his bum.

"It's bad news," Bubbles translated. "This is a very big job."

The builder unfurled a blueprint of the house. Professor Utonium studied it carefully. "It looks like the whole house needs underpinning before we can attempt reconstruction," he said.

"Dude, what does that mean?" Buttercup asked.

"It means we need to move," said the Professor sadly.

"Move!" gasped The Powerpuff Girls.

"But this is our home," whimpered Bubbles.

Professor Utonium patted her gently on the head. "I know it's sad," he said. "But I'm sure there are plenty of other houses with a built-in science laboratory and a superhero base in the bedroom."

Hmmm. I wouldn't be so sure about that, Professor.

"In the meantime," said the Professor, "we can camp. It will be fun!"

The Powerpuff Girls flew to the back garden and folded the enormous piece of toast in half, making it into a tent. They filled it with pieces of furniture salvaged from the house.

"This will do nicely until we find a new home," said Professor Utonium.

"It's actually kind of cool," said Buttercup, perching on a chair missing one leg. It collapsed under her and she fell on to her bottom. "Ow!"

"I like camping," said Bubbles. "We're closer to animals." Her voice wobbled as she whispered, "Like bears ... and wolves ..."

Blossom shuddered as she tidied up the tent. "So. Much. Dirt."

The Powerpuff Girls huddled in the toast tent miserably. It was going to be a long night …

The next day, The Powerpuff Girls went to school as usual. But they all felt downhearted. In art class, Bubbles drew a picture of their big white house and started crying. Her tears smudged the picture, making her cry even harder. Buttercup was too sad to make rude jokes, even though they were learning about Uranus in science class. Even Blossom couldn't concentrate on her lessons. She got an A minus on her spelling test!

After school, the Mayor called The Powerpuff Girls for help. There was a dragon in Townsville – and he was hungry!

 The Powerpuff
Girls flew to
the rescue.

"Take that,"
said Buttercup, sighing sadly as she
punched the monster.

"Go us," Bubbles said, listlessly hitting
the monster.

The Powerpuff Girls booted the monster
into the sky and sent it flying back to
Monster Island.

"Whoopee," said Blossom
unenthusiastically.

"Want some pickles to celebrate
Townsville not being destroyed?" asked the
Mayor. The Powerpuff Girls weren't in the
mood for pickles – or for celebration.

"Nah," said Buttercup.

"No thank you, Mayor," said Blossom. "We'll just head home."

"Except we don't have a home any more!" wailed Bubbles.

Blossom knew they had to snap out of their superhero-sized bad mood. Back at the toast tent, she gathered her sisters round. "It really stinks that our house was destroyed," she said.

"Tell us something we don't already know," grumbled Buttercup.

"But maybe we should see this as an opportunity to find a new house that's *even* better," said Blossom. She got out a flip chart and a marker. "For instance, I've always dreamed of having a walk-in stationery closet." Blossom wrote 'stationery closet' on the flip chart.

"Ooh!" squealed Bubbles. "I want a petting zoo!"

Blossom added 'petting zoo' to the chart.

"What about you, Buttercup?" Blossom asked.

"Hmm," said Buttercup. "A shooting range in the basement would be pretty cool."

"OK," said Blossom, writing down 'shooting range'. "Let Operation Codename: Dream House begin!"

DREAM
HOUSE

> *The Powerpuff Girls were fast asleep, dreaming about their new house. In case you're interested, my dream house has an indoor pool and a chocolate fountain …*

"Bullseye!" Buttercup mumbled sleepily, dreaming about her shooting range.

Bubbles turned over and cuddled Octi, murmuring about monkeys and llamas.

"Rise and shine!" said Blossom, shaking her sisters awake. She handed them each a sheet of paper.

"What's this?" asked Buttercup, yawning and rubbing her eyes.

"It's a schedule," Blossom explained. "I've lined up several houses for us to look at today."

"I thought we could check out the old army base," said Buttercup. "It has lots of potential."

"That ugly building surrounded by barbed wire?" said Bubbles. "I couldn't have a petting zoo there – the bunnies' fur might get caught in the barbed wire!"

"Not if you tell them to stay away from it," said Buttercup. One of Bubbles' special powers was the ability to speak to animals.

"I think we should move to a farmhouse," said Bubbles dreamily. "With fields for the animals to play in—"

"Let's just stick to my schedule," interrupted Blossom. "I even created a handy rating system."

"Who died and made you in charge, Blossom?" said Buttercup, glaring at her sister.

"Fine!" said Blossom. "If you don't want to follow my carefully planned itinerary, we'll have to settle this a different way."

"Arm wrestling?" suggested Buttercup hopefully.

"A tickle fight?" said Bubbles.

"No!" said Blossom.

"Rock, Paper, Scissors!"

> *Oh dear. This could get ugly. The superhero version of Rock, Paper, Scissors is a bit rougher than the normal game. I'm going to make myself a cup of tea. You might want to get on with your knitting or read a book. Oh wait, you ARE reading a book ... anyway, let's leave them to it for a minute, you don't need to see this ...*
>
> *... that should do it.*

"Ha!" laughed Buttercup triumphantly. "Rock wins!"

"Well, don't blame me when you start wishing we'd stuck to a schedule," Blossom grumbled, straightening her hair bow.

"Breakfast time!" called Professor Utonium. "Toast, anyone?"

"Too soon," Buttercup said, groaning.

After breakfast, The Powerpuff Girls flew to the army base. A razor-sharp fence surrounded an enormous concrete bunker. There was a look-out tower with guns mounted on top.

"Oh yeah," said Buttercup. "Now *that's* what I call security!"

"That's what I call horrible," muttered Blossom.

Buttercup led them inside the bunker. She knocked on the drab grey walls approvingly. "These walls must be about a metre thick."

"Maybe they'd look nicer if we painted them blue," suggested Bubbles.

They went down some concrete stairs to the underground command centre. "Awesome," cried Buttercup, excitedly flying over to look at a huge control panel. "There's even a laser-guided missile system."

She pointed at a massive screen showing radar maps and satellite images.

"Too bad there aren't any windows," said Blossom, shivering. It was cold and damp in the basement.

"Who needs natural light when you've got lasers?" said Buttercup. "I wonder what this does?" She pressed a button and a red light flashed overhead. Suddenly an alarm blared out.

"What's that?" Bubbles shouted.

"TEN SECONDS TO MISSILE LAUNCH," a robotic voice announced.

"Oops!" Buttercup said.

Bubbles quickly reprogrammed the computer to de-activate the missile, and the alarm turned off. "I think we should keep looking."

"My turn!" Bubbles sang out excitedly. She led the others straight to a big old farmhouse with animals everywhere. Buttercup read out the sign: "Kuddly Kritters Animal Sanctuary."

"Isn't it perfect?" Bubbles squealed. Cats rubbed against the girls' legs while dogs ran around them in circles, yapping excitedly. There were donkeys munching grass, chickens pecking at the ground and a pair of ferrets racing up and down a plastic tunnel.

"Ugh," said Blossom. "This place smells worse than Buttercup's feet."

There were even more animals inside the farmhouse.

The kitchen was filled with food and water bowls and the living room had scratching posts and dog beds instead of furniture.

"There aren't any bedrooms," said Buttercup.

"That doesn't matter," said Bubbles, showing her sisters a big rabbit hutch. "We can all snuggle up with the bunnies. It will be cosy!"

"No way!" said Blossom. "It's totally unhygienic!" A parakeet flew across the room and pooped on her shoulder. "Eww!" she screamed, desperately wiping it off.

"It's supposed to bring you good luck when a bird does that," Bubbles told her happily.

But Blossom didn't look the slightest bit happy about her good fortune.

"I think Blossom's had all the good luck she can handle," Buttercup said, smothering a laugh.

"Fine!" said Bubbles. She set down the kitten she was cuddling and turned to Blossom. "Let's go see where YOU want to live."

The Powerpuff Girls flew to Midway Elementary School. "Ta da!" announced Blossom.

"Dude, I think you made a mistake," said Buttercup. "We're supposed to be looking for a new house, not going to school."

"I don't make mistakes," said Blossom smugly. "There's an empty classroom we could move into."

"Um ..." said Bubbles.

"Er ..." said Buttercup.

"I can tell you're speechless!" Blossom said smugly. "We'd *never* be late for school! Not that I ever am."

"It's bad enough that I have to go to school five days a week," shouted Buttercup. "I AM NOT LIVING HERE!"

"We can't take pets to school," Bubbles reminded Blossom.

Blossom sighed. Operation Codename: Dream House wasn't going very well. House hunting was much harder than she had thought it would be …

Meanwhile, across town, two very trendy criminals, Barbarus 'Barbie' and Bianca Bikini – otherwise known as The Fashionistas – were plotting to destroy The Powerpuff Girls. Because evil NEVER goes out of style!

"Did you see the news, Barbie?" asked Bianca Bikini, waving a newspaper at her sister. "The Powerpuff Girls' house was wrecked by a piece of toast. That's why I always avoid carbs!"

Today Bianca Bikini is wearing a short black dress with a darling little red belt, her black hair in a bun, white earrings, purple eye shadow and long, black false eyelashes.

Barbarus Bikini grunted in reply.

Barbie is wearing a black bikini, her blonde hair is swept into an updo and she's accessorised with a pearl bracelet and multiple rings. She also happens to be a gorilla.

"They'll be looking for a new house," said Bianca. "And who better to help them

than the most stylish sisters in Townsville?"

Barbie nodded in delight, then put her huge hairy arm around her sister.

"Quite right, Barbie," Bianca continued.

"We'll do our very best to help The Powerpuff Girls find their perfect dream house," she said with a sinister smile. "Or should I say, their **NIGHTMARE** house!"

> *DUN DUN DUUUUUN!*
> *That doesn't sound good, does it?*

A SNEAKY PLAN

Unaware that The Fashionistas were plotting their destruction, The Powerpuff Girls carried on house hunting.

"I've got a good feeling about this one," said Blossom to her sisters as they hiked up an icy mountainside.

"You said that about the last one," said Bubbles.

"And the one before that," said Buttercup.

Blossom checked the address on her phone. "We're here." She gazed around, but the only house in sight was a fairytale palace made of ice.

"I guess my petting zoo could have arctic hares," said Bubbles. "And maybe some penguins …"

"You said the army bunker was too cold," said Buttercup. "But this house is *literally* freezing. Ice palaces might look good in the movies, but you wouldn't want to live in one."

Blossom sighed. So far that day they'd looked at a leaky houseboat and a haunted

house full of ghosts. She'd thought a house near the railroad tracks might be the one until a train rumbled past. It shook the house so hard that all the pictures fell off the walls!

Discouraged, The Powerpuff Girls headed home. As they flew into Townsville, a billboard caught Blossom's eye. "Look!" she cried, stopping so suddenly that Bubbles and Buttercup crashed into her.

"Ouchie!" cried Bubbles, rubbing her nose.

The billboard showed a picture of a gorgeous mansion with a big garden. Above the picture it said:

LOOKING FOR YOUR DREAM HOUSE?
B & B ESTATE AGENTS WILL HELP YOU FIND IT!

"That house looks perfect!" said Blossom.

"There's definitely enough space for a petting zoo," said Bubbles.

"What are you waiting for?" asked Buttercup. "Call them!"

Blossom telephoned B&B Estate Agents. "Hello," she said. "Is the house on your billboard still available?"

"Why, yes it is," purred the estate agent. "Let me just find the details. Here we are! It's a tastefully decorated four-bedroom house with oodles of storage space."

"That sounds good," said Blossom.

"There's a gym," the lady continued, "and a library and – this is really quite

unique – a purpose-built science laboratory."

"A science lab!" shrieked Blossom. "I think this might be our dream house! When can we see it?"

"I'll meet you there," the estate agent said, giving her the address.

Blossom hung up and grinned at her sisters. "I've got a good feeling about this one."

"For once I agree with you," said Buttercup.

As soon as she got off the phone, Bianca crowed with delight.

That's right – B&B Estate Agents are Bianca and Barbie! The Powerpuff Girls are walking right into a trap!

45

"Our billboard reeled them in, exactly as planned," Bianca said with a laugh. "This is almost too easy!"

Barbie grunted and scratched her blonde wig.

"You're right, Barbie," Bianca said. "We'll need a disguise."

The last time The Fashionistas had tried to take over Townsville, they had ended up in Albatross Prison, thanks to The Powerpuff Girls. Bianca had no intention of ever going back. Orange prison jumpsuits were NOT a good look for her!

"We'll wear something from last season," Bianca told Barbie. "That way they'll never guess it's us."

Bianca rummaged in the wardrobe and flung a short, hot-pink dress at her sister.

The ape put the dress on over her black bikini.

"You look divine, Barbie," cooed Bianca. "They'll never see through that disguise."

Bianca wriggled out of her sleek black dress and into a dark navy one. "Blue is the new black," she tittered.

When they were dressed, Bianca and Barbie admired themselves in a full-length mirror. "Are we forgetting anything?" said Bianca.

Barbie grunted and pointed to their reflections in the mirror.

"Of course! Accessories!" cried Bianca. "An outfit is never complete without fabulous accessories." She handed Barbie a pair of sunglasses, then grabbed a handbag that matched her dress and put a long scarf

around her face so that the girls wouldn't recognise her.

"Right!" she said. "Now we're dressed for distress!"

> *Bianca and Barbie looked like a million dollars in their dresses. Or rather, like they could STEAL a million dollars!*

When The Powerpuff Girls arrived at the mansion, they didn't notice the two odd-looking estate agents. They were too busy looking at the enormous white mansion. It looked even better than it had in the picture.

"Helloooo," said Bianca, air kissing Blossom, Bubbles and Buttercup. "Please excuse my scarf, girls, I have a terrible cold. But you're here to see your dream house,

not me," she said with a tinkly laugh. "As you can see, the property is EXTREMELY secure."

She pressed a button and heavy gold gates swung open. "It's VERY hard to get in," she said to the girls. "Or out!" she whispered to Barbie.

As they walked up the drive towards the big white mansion, Bianca started talking about the house. "The swimming pool is in the back, the science lab has its own separate wing, and there's a heli-pad on the lawn."

"Wow!" gasped Bubbles.

"Awesome!" said Buttercup.

The house was very impressive, but Blossom felt nervous for some reason. The two estate agents seemed familiar, but she couldn't figure out how she knew them.

"Do come inside," said Bianca, ushering them into the house.

In the living room, there were crystal chandeliers, fluffy rugs and leather sofas. Best of all, there was a television the size of a cinema screen!

"It's 3D," said Bianca, switching the TV on. A robot from *Space Towtruck* jumped out at them.

"I think I've gone to heaven," sighed Buttercup, sinking down on the sofa.

"Oh, but you must see the bedrooms," said Bianca, leading them upstairs.

The first bedroom was decorated in shades of pink. There were bookshelves, an executive-style desk with a computer, and a walk-in closet divided into separate sections.

"Ooooh," said Blossom, picturing her clothes hanging neatly inside it.

The second bedroom was painted a pretty pale blue, with lots of cute animal posters decorating the walls. Wooden letters

over the bed spelled out 'Bubbles'.

"This one has my name all over it," said Bubbles happily.

The third bedroom was green, with camouflage-print curtains and a basketball hoop mounted to the wall.

Buttercup flopped on to the bed. "I feel at home already."

"Don't get too comfy," said Bianca. "There's so much more to see! I haven't shown you the puppy parlour *or* the armoured garage yet."

"Puppy parlour?" gasped Bubbles.

"Armoured garage!" shouted Buttercup.

"Why don't you two go with my colleague," Bianca suggested, arching a perfectly groomed eyebrow. "Run down and see the puppy parlour and the garage."

Bubbles and Buttercup eagerly followed Barbie out of the room.

Blossom eyed Bianca suspiciously. The house was perfect. It could have been made for them. So why did she feel so uneasy?

Bianca smiled winningly at Blossom. "And how would you like a tour of the stationery suite?" she asked her.

"Stationery suite?" echoed Blossom, her eyes growing even wider than usual.

"Follow me!" said Bianca, leading Blossom downstairs into a room stuffed full of stationery.

There were notebooks with every type of paper. There was every type of writing implement imaginable – from felt tips and fountain pens to pencils, oil paints and pastels – in every shade of the rainbow!

There were piles of paper clips, stacks of
sticky notes and rows of rubbers and rulers.
Blossom breathed in the delicious aroma of
ink and glue and thought she might swoon.

"Take your time exploring," said Bianca,
shutting the door behind her. Turning the
lock, she hissed, "Because you're never
leaving!"

I didn't see that coming. OK, maybe I did.

Suddenly, Blossom realised why the
estate agents seemed so familiar. "They're
The Fashionistas!" she gasped.

PUPPIES!

Blossom was more stuck than a roll of double-sided super-sticky tape. But her sisters had no idea they were walking into a trap ...

"I can't believe there's a puppy parlour!" squealed Bubbles. "I mean, I've dreamed of a house with a room full of puppies, but I didn't know they actually existed!"

Barbie Bikini grunted as she led Bubbles and Buttercup through the mansion.

"What kind of puppies are there?" Bubbles asked her. "Labradors are probably my favourite breed, but pugs and poodles are super cute too."

Again, Barbie just grunted.

"Not exactly chatty, is she?" Buttercup whispered to Bubbles.

But Bubbles was so excited, she couldn't stop babbling. "I also really love bassets and beagles and boxers ..."

At last Barbie pushed a door open. Bubbles gasped, dazed by the sight that met her big blue eyes. There were black puppies with long, silky tails and white puppies with short, stubby tails. There were spaniels with curly hair and sheepdogs with shaggy hair.

There were tiny terriers and big bulldogs. Everywhere Bubbles looked there were puppies, puppies and more PUPPIES!

"I ... can't ... even ..." said Bubbles. She sank to the floor, arms open wide. Puppies swarmed around her, wagging their tails

and yipping in delight. Bubbles giggled as a golden retriever puppy licked her face.

"You are sooooo gorgeous," she squealed, giving him a cuddle.

"My sister really likes puppies," Buttercup explained to Barbie.

A tiny Chihuahua puppy with enormous eyes and huge ears went up to Barbie and growled. Then it cocked its leg and piddled against the Fashionista's hairy pink leg. Barbie jumped back with a roar.

Suddenly, Bianca Bikini swept into the puppy parlour. "Oh no!" she gasped, staring at the yellow puddle on her sister's shoes. "Those are genuine crocodile leather!"

"If ya gotta go, ya gotta go," said Buttercup, shrugging.

Bianca gave Buttercup a fake smile. "Why don't we leave your sister to get acquainted with her furry friends," Bianca said, "while I show *you* the armoured garage."

"Good idea," said Buttercup. The Puppy Parlour was beginning to smell.

Bubbles was too busy patting the puppies to notice the odour – or the fact that everyone was leaving.

"Heh, heh, heh," chuckled Barbie as she shut the door and turned a key in the lock. **CLICK!** Bubbles was locked inside!

> *Oh dear. Things are looking hairy for Bubbles. Really hairy – I mean, do you have any idea how much golden retrievers shed?*

The garage was a separate building next to the mansion.

"*Voila!*" cried Bianca, pressing a remote control. The garage door slowly opened, revealing a tank parked inside.

Buttercup couldn't believe her eyes.

Was this all just an amazing dream? She had wanted her very own tank like, for ever. For  once, she was lost for words.

"It's the newest model, with all the latest military technology," Bianca said. "Let's go and take a closer look."

Inside the garage, there were piles of ammunition ranging from small hand grenades to giant cannonballs. Shiny power tools hung from hooks on the wall and weapons were neatly stacked on racks. There was even a flamethrower!

Buttercup walked up to the tank and ran her hands over its caterpillar tracks, sighing lovingly.

"Go on!" urged Bianca. "Try sitting in it."

Buttercup climbed into the gun turret and pretended to fire. She almost wished there was a supervillain nearby so she could try it out.

Yoo hoo, Buttercup! Right in front of you!

"It's a perfect fit," Bianca said.

"I'm not sure if the Professor will let me have a tank," said Buttercup, climbing out of the turret. "He always says they're too dangerous."

"I'm sure he'll change his mind when he sees how good you look in it," purred Bianca, her eyes gleaming. "Why don't you have a little play here in the garage while I go and see how your sisters are getting on with the rest of the tour."

"Yeah, absolutely, south-facing garden," said Buttercup absently. She was completely distracted by the tank. "It has a crossbow AND a flamethrower!" she gasped.

Bianca quietly walked out of the garage and pressed the remote control again. But as the garage door swung down, she chortled with glee. "All three sisters exactly where I want them!" she laughed. "Now let's see how they like being put in prison for once!"

Bianca and Barbie met in the only room they hadn't shown The Powerpuff Girls – the control chamber.

There were three screens. One showed Blossom in the stationery suite. Another showed Bubbles sitting in the puppy parlour, surrounded by cuddly canines.

The last one showed Buttercup in the
garage.

"Their stupid dresses might actually be in
style by the time they get out," Bianca said,
jabbing a button. Then she laughed and
said, "Who am I kidding? Those dresses will
NEVER be fashionable and The Powerpuff
Girls will NEVER get out!"

In the stationery suite, heavy metal bars
dropped down in front of the doorway. **CLANG!**

"Oh no!" Blossom gasped.

In the garage, steel bars slammed down in
front of the remote-controlled door. **THUNK!**

"Oh no!" Buttercup cried, looking up
from the torpedo she was polishing.

In the puppy parlour, metal bars crashed
down in front of the door, narrowly missing a
poodle's pom-pom tail. **SLAM!**

Bubbles was nuzzling noses with a fluffy white puppy. "I love puppies!" she said, giggling. Then she looked up and saw the bars. "I mean, oh no!"

POWERPUFF PRISON

> *The Powerpuff Girls' perfect rooms had become perfect prisons. I wonder how their plans for a jail break are coming along …*

Blossom had completely reorganised the stationery suite, with paper products on one side of the room and pens, pencils and paints arranged by colour on the other side.

Blossom was in the special 'Chill Out' zone with several different sizes of stapler.

"Stay calm, Blossom," she told herself, stapling sheet after sheet of paper. Stapling always soothed her. Soon, she had stapled a stack of papers nearly as tall as herself. The staples were all jauntily positioned in the top left-hand corner, in her signature style.

"You need a plan," Blossom told herself. Luckily, there was no shortage of stationery to help her. She chose a notebook with a pink cover.

"Plan A," Blossom wrote neatly in biro and then underlined it with a pink highlighter. "Use superhuman strength to bend the bars."

Carefully recapping her highlighter so it didn't dry out, Blossom went over to the

prison bars and tried to pull them apart.

"Urrghhh!" she grunted, her face red
with exertion as she tried to pry the metal
bars apart with her super-strong arms. But it
was no use – the bars didn't budge.

Blossom didn't panic. She nibbled on

the end of her pen for a moment. Then she wrote "Plan B: Use laser vision to burn through the bars."

Blossom narrowed her eyes. Bright red laser beams shot out and hit the bars. But the light ricocheted harmlessly off the metal.

"Hmm," Blossom said, blinking. "That's unusual." She always had a Plan B in case Plan A didn't work. But she didn't usually need a Plan C …

Blossom still didn't panic. She thought again and calmly wrote "Plan C: Use aura to break through the bars."

Blossom concentrated hard. Pink light glowed out of her and took the shape of a staple gun. Her aura quivered in the air then fired staples at the bars. They bounced

off the metal bars
with loud pings.

Blossom went
back to the "Chill Out"
zone. She started stapling
sheets of paper – and not in the top left-hand
corner! "I," she said. **STAPLE!** "Don't." **STAPLE!**
"Have." **STAPLE!** "Any." **STAPLE!** "Other." **STAPLE!**
"Plans!" **STAPLE, STAPLE, STAPLE, STAPLE!**

Now Blossom was panicking!

*Let's leave Blossom to her stapling. Maybe
Bubbles is having more luck …*

In the puppy parlour, Bubbles was trying
to think of a way out too, but she was finding
it hard to concentrate surrounded by so
much cuteness! Besides, the puppies didn't
want her to think – they wanted her to play!

71

"Fetch, boy!" she called, throwing a tennis ball across the room for what felt like the gazillionth time. Her arm was beginning to ache!

A chocolate brown retriever ran right back to her and dropped the tennis ball at her feet, wagging its tail.

"Good boy," Bubbles said, stroking the puppy's head.

A Dalmatian puppy pawed Bubbles' leg and whimpered.

"Hi there, Spotty," Bubbles said, giving the puppy a pat. "What do you want?"

The puppy piddled on the floor. "Oh, *that's* what you want," said Bubbles, sighing. "At least it wasn't a number two."

The Puppy Parlour was getting really stinky. Bubbles wanted to get out – and so

did all the puppies!

"Listen up, guys," she told the puppies. They gathered around and pricked up their ears. "I'm going to take you all for walkies as soon as I break down these bars."

Bubbles' singing voice was so loud and sweet it could shatter glass. She really hoped it would work on metal, too.

"*How much is that doggie in the window ...*" Bubbles sang at the top of her lungs. The puppies started to yip and yelp. "*The one with the waggly tail ...*" Now the puppies were howling and covering their ears with their paws.

Humans always found Bubbles' voice irresistible. But dogs have better hearing than humans, and it seemed the puppies didn't like her high-pitched singing!

Bubbles stopped singing and sighed. Then another puppy made a puddle on the floor.

"Actually, I need to go, too," Bubbles said, crossing her legs. Suddenly, she couldn't stop thinking of trickling streams and flowing rivers and waterfalls …

At this rate The Powerpuff Girls are going to be The Powerpuff Grannies by the time they escape. Surely Buttercup has figured out a way out …

Inside the garage, Buttercup was leaning against the tank and whistling to herself as she tossed a hand grenade up in the air and caught it.

She looked totally relaxed.

Okaaaaay. I'm sure Buttercup is busy, er, thinking.

Back in the control room, The Fashionistas were celebrating in their favourite way – with an online shopping spree! There were three different luxury shopping websites open on the computer screens.

"Those shoes are *literally* to die for," Bianca said, admiring a pair of spiky black stilettos. "The high heels will make perfect weapons. Let's each get a pair!" She clicked twice and added the shoes to her Glam-azon.com shopping basket.

Barbie grunted and pointed to a slinky black dress on her screen.

"Ooh! That little black dress will look so chic on you, Barbie," Bianca said. "And something for me, too," she said, choosing a diamond-encrusted watch. "Because it's *time* the The Fashionistas took over Townsville!" She laughed hysterically at her own joke.

"Don't worry, Barbie," she added as she typed in her credit card details. "I'm using a stolen credit card, of course."

Barbie grunted and pointed at the screens.

"I suppose we *should* check on the little brats," Bianca said. She pressed a button and the shopping websites were replaced with views of the three prisons. Speaking into a microphone she said, "Attention, Powerpuff Girls! The Fashionistas have put you under HOUSE arrest."

On the first screen, Blossom was surrounded by a mountain of stapled paper.

The second screen showed Bubbles slumped against a wall, puppies all over her.

"Ew!" said Bianca, shuddering. "Nobody wears fur any more!" Glancing at her hairy sister, she added, "No offence, darling."

On the third screen, Buttercup was waving at them.

"Oh, look!" Bianca chortled. "She's waving to us. As if we're going to save her!"

Buttercup was definitely waving, but she didn't appear to want help. In fact, she looked positively cheerful as she climbed into the tank and turned on the engine.

Maybe Buttercup does have a plan after all!

TANKTASTIC

The Fashionistas had locked Buttercup inside a garage with a tank. Can anyone else spot the teeny tiny flaw in their plan?

"Geronimo!" cried Buttercup and she drove the tank straight at the garage doors. She fired the tank's gun at the metal bars and burst through the armoured doors.

Buttercup was free!

"Woo hoo!" Buttercup cheered. "This is one sweet ride."

Buttercup steered the tank across the lawn and crashed through the mansion's front door. In the distance, she could hear barking. Following the sound, Buttercup drove the tank to where Bubbles was trapped.

"Stand back!" Buttercup shouted as the tank burst into the puppy parlour, flattening the metal bars.

"Can'tstopgottapeeeeeeee!" Bubbles yelled as she flew down the hallway to the luxurious marble bathroom, slamming the door behind her.

Aaah! That's a relief!

"Hurry up," said Buttercup when Bubbles came back. "We need to rescue Blossom."

"The puppies are coming with us," said Bubbles. She clipped on the puppies' leads and attached them to the door that Buttercup had broken down. Standing on the door, Bubbles yelled, "Walkies!" The puppies shot forwards, pulling the door along like a sleigh.

Buttercup drove the tank through the house, leaving muddy track marks all over the white carpets. Bubbles' dog sled bounded after it.

At the end of a corridor, the tank barged into the stationery suite, crushing a mountain of stapled paper under its tracks.

"Oh, thank goodness!" Blossom gasped. "I was running out of staples! I don't know what I would have done then."

"Yeah, that would have been a *real* disaster," Buttercup said sarcastically.

Blossom grabbed armfuls of stationery and shoved it into the tank's gun turret.

"Dude, this isn't the time to stockpile school supplies," said Buttercup impatiently. "We've got to stop The Fashionistas."

"This stuff always comes in handy," Blossom said, gathering as many rolls of tape as she could hold.

Plotline alert! Look out for those rolls of tape — I have a feeling we might see them again later!

Back in the control room, Bianca and Barbie were putting on their war paint, preparing to battle The Powerpuff Girls. Bianca angrily brushed her hair, then put on colourful eyeshadow and black mascara. "I just can't believe they got out," she grumbled.

Barbie scratched her head thoughtfully.

"Pucker up, sweetie," Bianca said, painting her sister's lips with bright red lipstick. She quickly snapped a selfie, tagging it #KillerLook.

Outside the mansion, The Powerpuff Girls – and lots of puppies – were waiting for The Fashionistas. It was handbags at, er, midday.

Bianca tried to pretend that they really were estate agents. "So, girls," she cooed.

"What do you think of the house? I bet you can't wait to move in!"

"YOU'RE the ones who are going to be moving," yelled Buttercup from the tank's gun turret. "Because we're sending you back to jail!"

"Never!" cried Bianca. "Anyway, I should call the fashion police on the three of you! Don't you ever wear anything but those tacky little dresses?"

"Our dresses aren't tacky," Bubbles said angrily. "They're CUTE!"

"And practical," added Blossom. "They're machine-washable and very comfortable for fighting in."

"And they have SECRET POCKETS," Buttercup said, bringing a hand grenade out of her pocket and flinging it at them. **BOOM!**

Bianca jumped out of the way just in time. "Barbie, be a doll and go and deal with them," said Bianca, giving her sister a shove. "I just had a manicure and don't want to chip a nail."

Barbie lumbered up to the tank and scaled it, waving her handbag like a weapon.

She swung the bag at Buttercup, who blocked it with her fist.

"Careful with that handbag, Barbie," shrieked Bianca. "It's designer!"

Barbie tried to clobber Blossom over the head but Blossom ducked out of the way and dived into the tank's gun turret.

As Barbie swung her handbag at Buttercup again, Blossom had an idea. She popped out of the turret brandishing a tape gun loaded with rainbow-striped sticky tape.

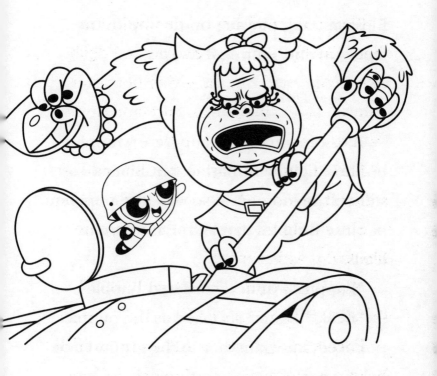

In a jiffy, the hairy pink ape was bound
tighter than a parcel.

"Nooooooo! Stripes are *so* not in this
season!" Bianca wailed.

"I knew this would come in handy!"

Blossom said, blowing on the top of the
tape gun and putting it away.

Told you we'd be seeing it again!

Blossom and Buttercup were wrapping
up their fight with Barbie, but Bianca was
still on the loose. And so were the puppies,
because Bubbles had let them off their
leads.

"Puppies – attack!" ordered Bubbles.

"Eeek!" Bianca shrieked as the puppies
pounced, knocking her to the ground and
licking her. "They're getting hair on my
dress!" she wailed, desperately trying to
escape from their slobbery kisses. "No!!!!"
she howled as a terrier pulled off one of
her shoes. "Give that back!" she ordered the
puppy. "These shoes cost a fortune!"

Well, they would have if she'd actually paid for them!

The puppy scampered across the lawn and started digging a hole to bury Bianca's designer shoe.

Bianca struggled to her feet and ran back to the control chamber. Barbie hopped after her, legs and arms bound tightly to her sides. Barbie made it inside and slammed the door.

"What are we going to do now? They could stay in there for weeks!" groaned Bubbles.

"Everyone into the tank!" Buttercup yelled. "We'll break down the door! It's tanking time!"

"No, wait, let's come up with a plan."
Blossom said. "We need to get The
Fashionistas to come out so that we can take
them back to jail for good, right?"

"But how?" asked Bubbles.

"What's the one thing The Fashionistas
can't resist?" Blossom asked her sisters.

"Being annoying?" said Buttercup.

"Puppies?" guessed Bubbles.

Blossom shook her head. "No," she said.
"A limited edition." Turning to Bubbles, she
said, "We're going to have to hack into the
Glam-azon.com website."

"No problem!" Bubbles said.

The girls sneaked upstairs to the pink
bedroom. Bubbles logged on to the
computer and quickly infiltrated the Glam-
azon.com website. She created a fake ad

for a limited edition, velvet-lined, diamond-studded evening bag.

"And now, we wait," Blossom said triumphantly.

Back in the control room, the Fashionistas were laughing. "It'll soon be their bedtime and those Powerpuff Girls will have to go home!" Bianca said delightedly.

Barbie grunted.

"Quite right!" Bianca replied. "There is just enough time for a spot of internet shopping!"

She logged into Glam-azon.com and squealed out loud as the ad for the bag popped up on the screen in front of her. "Have you ever seen something so stunning?" she gasped. "And it's ON SALE!"

Another ad for the bag popped up on screen, saying it was available at Boutique L'Orange.

"Quick, Barbie, we need to go NOW!" Bianca said. "It's a limited edition – and I'd kill for one."

Bianca and Barbie slowly opened the control room door. Outside, The Powerpuff Girls were lying on the living room sofas, fast asleep.

With a gleeful look at the sleeping superheroes, The Fashionistas ran out of the control room, jumped into the tank and sped away.

As soon as they heard the tank, The Powerpuff Girls opened their eyes and peered at the hastily departing criminals.

"That worked perfectly!" said Bubbles.

"They took my tank!" Buttercup cried.
"My beautiful tank!"

"Where is Boutique L'Orange exactly?"
Blossom asked Bubbles as The Fashionistas
disappeared. "I've never heard of it."

"That's because I made it up," said Bubbles, smiling sweetly. "The address they're heading to is Albatross Prison."

CRIME
DOESN'T PAY

> *The Fashionistas were heading back to jail and The Powerpuff Girls were free!*

"Way to go, Bubbs!" Buttercup said, giving her sister a high-five.

"It was easy," Bubbles said, shrugging modestly. "Glam-azon.com really should beef up their firewall."

Blossom looked around at the mess the battle had made. "I'd better get this place tidied up," she said. Her pink aura glowed and took the shape of a vacuum cleaner.

"You don't need to do that," said Buttercup, as Blossom vacuumed the carpet.

"Oh, I want to," Blossom said cheerfully. "There's something so satisfying about cleaning up a mess this big. Just look at all these muddy pawprints!"

"Um, speaking of muddy pawprints," said Bubbles, suddenly looking worried, "where have all the puppies gone?"

Buttercup quickly scanned the mansion's grounds with her laser vision. "They're in the garden next door," she told her.

"Phew!" said Bubbles. "Let's get them and take them home with us."

"Um, Bubbs," said Blossom. "I hate to point out the obvious, but we don't have a home."

"Oh no!" wailed Bubbles. "Where will the puppies live?"

"Maybe you can hack into Glam-azon. com again and sell them?" Buttercup suggested.

Bubbles was horrified by her sister's suggestion. "Puppies are NOT fashion accessories," she told Buttercup.

"That's not what I meant—" Buttercup started crossly, but Blossom interrupted her.

"We'll figure something out," Blossom assured Bubbles.

The Powerpuff Girls flew over the garden fence to the big brick house next door to the mansion.

As they got closer, they could hear laughter and barks of joy. The puppies were in the garden, romping happily with the children who lived there. Little toddlers were stroking the puppies, while older children were throwing balls and having tug-of-wars.

"Wow, this must be the biggest family ever," said Bubbles, staring at all the kids.

"It isn't a family," said Blossom. "They're orphans." She pointed to the sign on the building that read *Townsville Orphanage.*

"The puppies look so happy with all these kids to play with," said Bubbles. "Maybe they could live here?"

Blossom flew inside the orphanage and organised everything. When she came out, she had a huge smile. "They can live here for ever!" she told her sisters, happily.

"And best of all, there were exactly the right number of puppies for every orphan to have their own pet!"

What are the odds, eh?

"Yay!" said Bubbles. She went around giving each of the puppies a goodbye cuddle and promised to come and visit them soon.

As they flew back to Professor Utonium, Blossom turned to her sisters sadly. "I'm sorry I didn't find us a perfect home," she said.

"That's OK," said Buttercup. "I like camping."

"I just hope it doesn't rain," said Blossom. "I don't think that toast is waterproof."

"You know what," said Bubbles, "when I was stuck in the Puppy Parlour without the two of you I realised something."

"That white carpet isn't a good idea when you have puppies?" asked Blossom.

"NO," laughed Bubbles. "I realised that home isn't a specific place. It's wherever I am with my sisters and the Professor."

"That's right," said Blossom, nodding in agreement. "I don't need a stationery suite. Or even a stationery cupboard. I just need my family."

"True," said Buttercup. "But having a garage big enough for a tank would be pretty cool."

"Buttercup!" Blossom scolded her sister.

When she saw the look Bubbles and Blossom were giving her, Buttercup quickly added, "But not as cool as you guys."

"So Operation Codename: Dream House is over," said Blossom. "We'll tell the Professor that we don't need a dream house – we're happy to live anywhere, as long as we're together."

Bubbles and Buttercup nodded and smiled.

Home is where the heart is. But I prefer it when my heart has a roof over it.

Suddenly, Blossom shouted, "O.M.G!" She pointed at a big white house. "Look!" The house had a red door and three round windows. There was a garage on one side,

and a science lab on the other.

"So what?" said Bubbles. "It's our house." A second later it hit her. "IT'S OUR HOUSE!" she squealed. "IT'S FIXED!"

The Powerpuff Girls flew round the house in delight and landed in the garden.

Professor Utonium came out to greet them, followed by a robot that looked like a power drill crossed with a cement mixer.

"Did the builder fix our house?" asked Bubbles.

"No," said Professor Utonium, smiling. "I did."

"How?" asked Blossom, gazing at the house in wonder.

"When I saw how upset you girls were about the house," explained the Professor, "I knew I needed to do something. Some of the equipment in my lab was still usable, so I gathered some spare parts together and invented a special construction robot." The Professor patted the robot on its hard-hatted head. "It repaired the house in no time."

Blossom, Bubbles and Buttercup followed the Professor inside the house. Everything was exactly how it had been before the Toaster Monster destroyed it. In the living room, pictures were hanging on the walls. The television and the big red sofa were as good as new.

"This is amazing," said Buttercup.

"Oh good," said the Professor. "I was a bit worried that you girls might have wanted to redecorate."

"No," said Blossom. "As long as we're together, I don't want to change a thing."

"It's perfect just how it is," said Bubbles.

Buttercup nodded. Then she said, "Although if the garage was a tiny bit bigger, we could probably fit a tank in there …"

"Buttercup!" cried Blossom and Bubbles.

"Just kidding," said Buttercup, grinning. "We found our dream house after all!"

Once again, The Powerpuff Girls had saved the day – and learned that there truly is no place like home!

THE END

LOVE THIS POWERPUFF GIRLS ADVENTURE?

Then you'll love the next one EVEN MORE!
In HERO TO ZERO, Blossom, Bubbles and
Buttercup lose their powers. Without them,
they're just … puff girls. Can they get their
powers back AND save the day?

TURN OVER FOR A SNEAK PEEK!

SPECIAL DELIVERY

Some jobs are harder than others. Doctors, police officers, firefighters and writers work tirelessly to keep us safe. (OK, maybe not writers). But no one works harder than superheroes!

"I am soooooooo tired!" said Buttercup, flying into the bedroom she shared with her sisters. She dropped her school bag.

"Budge over, Bloss," she said, dive-bombing on to the bed next to Blossom and Bubbles.

"Sorry," groaned Blossom. "I can't move a muscle."

"I'm so tired I can't even blink," said Bubbles, staring up at the bedroom ceiling with her big blue eyes.

"It has been a busy week," said Blossom with a yawn. "We rescued the mayor from that gang of evil amoebas, we stopped a criminal mastermind from stealing Townsville's gold and then we fought off that army of mole men."

"Don't forget the out-of-control robot we took down," Buttercup reminded her. She rubbed her shoulder. It was still sore from punching the giant metal menace!

"Or that dragon monster we defeated," said Bubbles. "If it hadn't been for us he'd have burned down the whole town!"

"Sometimes I wish we weren't the only superheroes in Townsville," Buttercup said, sighing wearily.

"Maybe I'll just have a little nap," said Bubbles, cuddling her purple octopus toy, Octi.

"We can't take a nap," Blossom mumbled sleepily. "We've got tons of homework to do …"

That's right — superheroes have to do homework, too! The next time you complain about learning your times tables, count yourself lucky that you don't have to fight crime as well!

"I really need to catch some ZZZs," said Buttercup, yawning.

Her sisters didn't reply, because they had already nodded off.

But just as Buttercup's eyes shut, Professor Utonium called up the stairs. "Girls! There's post for you."

"Maybe it's a new stationery catalogue!" said Blossom, flying down the stairs in a blaze of pink light. She couldn't wait to browse through pages of highlighters, paper clips and notepads.

"I bet it's a letter from the panda I adopted," said Bubbles happily, trailing blue light as she zoomed after her sister.

"Dude, you know the panda isn't writing those letters, right?"

said Buttercup, rolling her eyes. "Besides, I'm expecting this month's edition of *Roller Derby Enthusiast* magazine." She strapped on her skates then zipped downstairs in a flash of green light.

Apparently The Powerpuff Girls did have a tiny bit of energy left, after all.

Professor Utonium handed them a brochure that had come in the post.

"*Villageton – A Greener Place to Live,*" said Blossom, reading the title out loud.
The girls flipped through the brochure, which had glossy photographs of the neighbouring town.

"I came all the way downstairs for this?" complained Buttercup.

"Oops, sorry," said Professor Utonium,

taking an envelope out of the pocket of his white lab coat. "This is what I meant to give you. It's addressed to all of you," he said.

"Oooh, just feel the quality of this paper," said Blossom, taking the thick, cream-coloured envelope.

"Who cares about the paper – what does it say?" grumbled Buttercup, snatching the envelope out of Blossom's hands and tearing it open. "The Mayor cordially invites you to the Annual Townsville Best Citizen of the Year Award ceremony," she read aloud. "Recognising the good deeds of Townsville's residents … blah, blah, blah," she said, tossing the letter aside.

"Wait!" cried Blossom. "Who's been nominated?" She grabbed the letter and scanned the list of nominees. "The Mayor's been nominated," she said.

"That's totally fair," said Buttercup sarcastically.

"And Dr Dee Kay," read Blossom. "For services to dentistry and oral hygiene."

"Get flossed," said Buttercup.

"Candy Honeydew has been nominated too," said Blossom. "She's a primary school teacher who spends her weekends picking up litter and volunteering for the Hats for Homeless Squirrels charity."

"Aw," said Bubbles. "That sounds like a really good cause. Squirrels are so cute!"

"Why do squirrels need hats?" grumbled Buttercup. "Don't they have fur on their heads?"

"There's one more nominee," said Blossom. "It's—" She blinked twice and passed the letter to Bubbles. "I'm so tired my eyes are playing tricks on me."

Bubbles read the letter and gasped. "Princess Morbucks?!"

Read

HERO TO ZERO

to find out what happens next!

SPOT THE DIFFERENCE

The Fashionistas are fiendish criminals, but they also love to look stylish! Can you spot the five differences between these images from their latest crime spree?

CALLING ALL PPG FANS!

What's Mojo Jojo's deepest secret?
Which villains are in a book club?
And which episode features a dancing panda?

Dazzle your friends with facts about
The Powerpuff Girls, play quizzes and games and find
out secret information about all your favourite characters in

THE POWERPUFF GIRLS OFFICIAL HANDBOOK!